THE ADVENTURES OF HARRY STEVENSON

Go, Go, Guinea Pig!

D1586021

THE ADVENTURES OF HARRY STEVENSON

Go, GO, Guinea Pig!

ALI PYE

SIMON & SCHUSTER

For Alex and Eddie,
Wilbur and Marnie

First published in Great Britain in 2021
by Simon & Schuster UK Ltd

Text, cover and interior illustrations copyright © 2021 Ali Pye

1 3 5 7 9 10 8 6 4 2

Simon & Schuster UK Ltd
1st Floor, 222 Gray's Inn Road, London WC1X 8HB

www.simonandschuster.co.uk
www.simonandschuster.com.au
www.simonandschuster.co.in

Simon & Schuster Australia, Sydney
Simon & Schuster India, New Delhi

A CIP catalogue record for this book is available from the British Library.

PB ISBN 978-1-4711-7027-0
EBook ISBN 978-1-4711-7028-7

Printed in China

STORY 1
It's showtime,
Harry Stevenson!

CHAPTER 1

What's up, Harry Stevenson?

Harry Stevenson was normally the happiest of guinea pigs. He had everything he could possibly want: a cosy cage full of hay and a food bowl that never seemed to empty. Even better, Harry lived with his favourite person in the world: eight-year-old Billy Smith. Billy was the best owner and friend a guinea pig could ask for. Today, though, Harry was feeling worried. That was because Billy was in a bad mood, and when Billy was unhappy, Harry was too.

The problem was Billy's cousin – Alfie. Harry had heard a lot about Alfie lately because he and his parents were coming to visit. According to Billy, his cousin was perfect in every way. He had all the latest toys, was brilliant at football and was always top of the class at school. *Alfie sounds great*, thought Harry, but it seemed he was wrong. For some reason, Billy didn't like Alfie very much. Harry couldn't work out why. Alfie sounded clever, sporty and fun – so why did Billy sigh when his parents talked about him? It was a big puzzle for a small guinea pig.

Harry Stevenson was a good friend, though, so while he couldn't understand Billy's bad mood, he was doing his best to improve it. The pair were curled up on the sofa in the front room. Their favourite football show was on TV but Harry could

tell that Billy wasn't really watching. He peered up at his friend – oh dear, there was that grumpy frown again. Harry nuzzled Billy's hand with his furry nose, then tried a cheery squeak. He was pleased to see a smile in response.

'Hey, Harry,' said Billy. 'At least Alfie hasn't got *you*. He's got everything else, it seems.' Billy was about to say more when Mrs Smith came into the room and spotted his glum face.

'Oh, Billy!' she said. 'Cheer up! I don't know what's got into you. Come on, love. Auntie Jen and Uncle Kevin will be here soon.'

Harry Stevenson chirped happily. He

loved Auntie Jen because she was just like her sister, Mrs Smith! Auntie Jen didn't visit very often as she lived in another city, but she always made a fuss of Harry when she came. Uncle Kevin was sort of fun too – although he kept pretending to think Harry was a 'ginger rat'. Harry got a bit tired of that joke sometimes. But Alfie? Harry had never met him. That was because Alfie had been playing in a football tournament when Auntie Jen visited, or performing in a dance show, or acting in a school play. It sounded like Alfie was good at *everything*, thought Harry, and he wondered again why Billy wouldn't admire such a clever cousin.

Harry looked at the door, hoping that Alfie,

Auntie Jen and Uncle Kevin would walk through it soon. They were just popping in before going to some sort of show, Mrs Smith had said. She didn't know any more than that – Auntie Jen had promised a surprise! Harry wasn't keen on surprises. He'd had a few lately and they *hadn't* been fun. Still, he always hoped for the best. Auntie Jen's surprise might involve nuggets, or, even better, carrots.

'They're here!' called Mrs Smith, looking out of the window excitedly. 'Ooh, that's the new car. Have a look, Billy!'

Billy shrugged, and carried Harry over to the window. Harry peered outside to see a big shiny car parking next to Mr Smith's

scruffy van. *I'd better smarten up*, thought Harry. So he gave himself a quick brush with his paws and prepared to meet the arrivals.

CHAPTER 2

Look at that,
Harry Stevenson!

Well, this IS a surprise, thought Harry
Stevenson, blinking in wonder. For standing
next to Auntie Jen and Uncle Kevin was a
boy who looked *just* like Billy! Harry knew
that Billy and Alfie were the same age but
he'd no idea they looked so similar. Alfie
was like a mirror of Billy. He even walked

the same way. Harry could spot one difference, though. Alfie seemed sort of . . . shinier. His shoes weren't scuffed like Billy's, and everything he wore looked neat. Harry sniffed the air. *Mmm*. Alfie's clothes had a fresh, zingy smell. Billy's things only smelled like that when they'd first been washed.

'Hey, Alfie!' cried Mrs Smith, giving her nephew a hug. 'How's the football going? We heard your team's doing really well.'

'Oh, not bad,' shrugged Alfie. But before he could finish, Auntie Jen and Uncle Kevin were telling everyone about Alfie's team: how they'd reached the final of a big competition, and how Alfie had scored in every game. Harry heard Billy sigh. Billy's team had lost a lot of matches recently.

'How's the new school, Billy?' asked Uncle Kevin.

'Er, OK, thanks,' Billy mumbled.

'Alfie LOVES school, don't you, Alf?' said Uncle Kevin, patting his son on the back. 'He's on the school council *and* in the top group for maths!'

Harry took a quick glance at his friend. Billy didn't like maths at all – he was always telling Harry how hard it was. Sure enough, a strange look passed across Billy's face. The look lasted just a second, though, before Billy blinked it away – so only Harry noticed.

'And how do you like your new flat, Billy?' said Auntie Jen. 'It's lovely, isn't it?'

'It's great,' agreed Billy.

'You must come and stay with us,' smiled Auntie Jen. 'Alfie's room is big enough for both of you, and he's got lots of new toys. We've got a trampoline and goalposts in the garden too!'

Ooh! thought Harry. The Smiths didn't

have goalposts – or a trampoline, whatever that was. Harry was impressed!

'Yes, come and have a kick about!' said Uncle Kevin. 'You'll play better than Sparky FC have done lately, hey?' he teased. 'Alfie's a Scratchy United fan. They thrashed the Sparks last week. Didn't they, Alf?'

Alfie nodded and gave a little smile.

Oh dear, thought Harry, looking at Billy's cross face. He knew how much Billy loved Sparky FC and hated being teased about them! Harry chuntered angrily, making Uncle Kevin smile.

'Sorry, Billy,' he said. 'I didn't spot your ginger rat! How's Harry Stevenson these days? We've brought something special to show him. You won't BELIEVE it when you see it!'

And Uncle Kevin was right!

Alfie went into the entrance hall of the flat
and came back carrying a bag and a smart-
looking box. Harry Stevenson gazed at the
box. It was the same shape as Harry's plastic
pet carrier but a lot fancier. Interesting. But
what could be inside?

Harry sniffed the air again. *Sniff, sniff,
sniff . . .*

OOHHHH!

No, thought Harry Stevenson. *It can't be.*

Harry felt more and more excited as Alfie
put the box down on the Smiths' kitchen
table and rootled about inside. He nearly
wheeked out loud when something rustled

in the carrier. Alfie caught whatever it was in the box and prepared to bring it out. Harry held his breath. His whiskers quivered.

'Everyone,' said Alfie, lifting his hands out of the carrier. 'Meet Monty.'

'WHEEK, WHEEK, WHEEEK; OH, WHEEK, WHEEK, WHEEK!' cried Harry Stevenson madly, as he stared and stared . . . into eyes just like his own!

Harry heard Billy gasp. Mr and Mrs Smith were so surprised they were lost for words. Mr Smith even spilled his tea and biscuits!

'Blimey,' spluttered Mr Smith eventually, brushing crumbs off his trousers. 'It's a guinea pig! And it's the spitting image of Harry!'

CHAPTER 3

TWO of you, Harry Stevenson?

Harry was so keen to see his lookalike that he scrabbled about in Billy's arms, trying to get a better view. *There must be SOMETHING that makes us different*, he thought. But, no: Monty was a perfect match to Harry, from the furry tuft on his head to his fluffy ginger bottom.

I'm not sure I like this, thought Harry. *I prefer it when there's just one of me!*

Monty didn't seem too happy about things either. Harry was about to say hello with a friendly **wheek**, when Monty gave him a look that stopped that **wheek** in its tracks. Monty stared at Harry, gave a sniff and wrinkled up his nose like he'd smelled something bad. Then he chattered his teeth in an unfriendly manner, before turning his head away from Harry and ignoring him.

How rude, thought Harry! But poor Harry: worse was to come.

'They could be twins, couldn't they?' said Uncle Kevin. 'The thing is, though, Monty's *really* clever.'

Hey! thought Harry Stevenson. *I'm clever too!*

'Alfie's been training Monty to do tricks,' explained Auntie Jen proudly. 'He's been doing it every day after school. The pair of them have got really good, so they started entering pet shows. It grew and grew and now they've reached the final of *Super-Pets* – you know, that talent show on TV where people do routines with their pets. It's filming this afternoon: that's why we're in town.'

SUPER-PETS! thought Harry. *We LOVE that show!* It was true – the Smiths snuggled up on the sofa every week to watch it. They weren't the only ones – Harry had heard Billy and his friends talking non-stop about the talented animals on the show. He'd also spotted lots of articles about it, in the newspapers lining his cage. It seemed like the whole country had gone mad for *Super-Pets.*

'That's AMAZING!' cried Mrs Smith. 'Isn't it, Billy?' But to Harry's surprise Billy didn't answer, and stared stonily ahead.

'Go on, Alfie. Show them your tricks!' urged Uncle Kevin.

Alfie looked a bit embarrassed, but pleased too.

'OK, then,' he said, and set to work.

Everyone gathered round as Alfie carefully placed the contents of his bag on the floor. Mr and Mrs Smith *oohed* and *aahed* as Alfie showed off each item. Most of them were tiny versions of things Harry recognized: a teeny ball, a mini skateboard, some little jumps like the ones in horse races on TV, and a toy-sized basketball hoop. There were also random things like a matchbox and a bangle.

Alfie set Monty down and the show started. First of all, Alfie held up his hand. Then Monty stood on his back legs and high-fived him!

'*WOW!*' cried Mr and Mrs Smith. But Harry wasn't impressed. *I'm sure* I *could do that . . . if I wanted to*, he thought.

The show continued.

'Turn around, Monty,' said Alfie, drawing circles in the air with his finger. Monty spun around as he followed Alfie's hand.

I'm pretty sure I could do that too, huffed Harry. He looked up to see what his friend thought, but Billy was staring out of the window. *Whatever Billy's looking at must be very interesting*, thought Harry, *because he's missing Monty's display!*

Next Alfie held out the matchbox and Monty pulled out the tray, revealing a nugget inside! *Um, I think I could do that . . . if I tried*, mused Harry. *I could* DEFINITELY *eat that nugget – much quicker than Monty.*

But Monty's tricks came thick and fast, and even Harry had to admit they were something special. He watched in awe as Monty pulled the bangle off Alfie's arm with his teeth, whizzed along on the little skateboard, skilfully pushed the ball around a box, then picked it up in his mouth and dropped it neatly into the basketball hoop.

Finally Monty scampered round an obstacle course, leaping over the little jumps with a distinctly smug look on his furry face!

Harry felt strangely glum. Mr and Mrs Smith clapped and clapped. Billy sighed a little sigh, but only Harry heard.

'Can Harry do any tricks?' asked Uncle Kevin, turning to face Billy. 'Some of them are quite simple. Why not have a try?'

Poor Billy looked as if he might explode! *Now I understand*, thought Harry Stevenson, finally realizing how Billy felt about his cousin. It seemed that everything Billy could do, Alfie could do better. And, oh dear, it looked like the same went for their pets!

CHAPTER 4

Smile, Harry Stevenson!

Soon it was time for Uncle Kevin and Auntie Jen to head off. They needed to drive to the TV centre where *Super-Pets* was being filmed.

'Let's have a photo of the boys and their guinea pigs,' said Auntie Jen, reaching for her phone.

Uncle Kevin looked at his watch. 'Better make it quick,' he said. 'It'll take a while to get across town and we can't keep the audience waiting.'

The boys sat next to each other on the sofa, guinea pigs on their laps. Harry Stevenson had had enough of Monty and didn't even want to *look* at him, so he turned away and left his furry bottom to face the visitors.

Then Monty lunged at that bottom and bit it, hard!

'WHEEEK!!!!' cried Harry in surprise. That stung! Keen to avoid another nip, he leaped off Billy's lap and on to the floor, but Monty followed fast behind. Teeth chattering, Harry fled under the sofa. It was dark there, with lots of places to hide. Harry spotted one of Mrs Smith's slippers, an empty box of chocolates and a newspaper. He scuttled to and fro as Monty chased him around, then dived under the newspaper and trembled.

From his hiding place, Harry could hear the humans debating what to do. There wasn't much of a gap under the sofa – it was so low they had to lie on the floor to see underneath. The adults' arms were too wide to fit under and the children's were too short to stretch to the back, so no one could reach the guinea pigs. Harry's ears pricked up when Mr Smith suggested luring them out with treats, but Uncle Kevin was in too much of a hurry to try.

'Come on,' he said, sounding worried. 'We can't be late! Let's lift the sofa up. Billy and Alfie: you reach underneath and try and catch them.'

Harry Stevenson's nose started to twitch as the sofa was lifted up and away. Light flooded on to big fluffy piles of dust that had been hidden underneath. So much of the dust was stuck to Harry's fur that he didn't look ginger any more.

Aaaach-CHOO, he sneezed. Harry glanced towards Monty who was also covered in dust. There were even a few bits of cereal stuck to his fur!

'Oh, no. That's just what we need,' groaned Uncle Kevin. 'Those guinea pigs look like they've been in a bin!' He sighed and clapped his hand to his head. 'Oh, well, no time to clear up now. We're on live TV in two hours! Just grab Monty, Alfie. Come on, quick!'

Harry Stevenson was fed up with cowering in the dust under a newspaper. It wasn't very nice, and now his nose was twitching as he felt another sneeze coming. *Ugh*, thought Harry. *Get me out of here!* So when a pair of hands came towards him, he didn't run away. Instead, he simply stepped on to them. Harry felt safe when the hands closed around him, and he shut his eyes with relief. *Thank you, Billy.* He felt himself being carried across the room and placed in some hay. Then Harry did what he always did after anything exciting happened: he started to feel sleepy.

As Harry nodded off, he heard Alfie worrying about his dusty guinea pig. 'Never mind,' Auntie Jen was saying. 'We can clean him up at the TV centre.'

Then everyone said goodbye, and Harry fell into a lovely, deep sleep.

CHAPTER 5

What's going on, Harry Stevenson?

Harry Stevenson awoke in a nest of soft, cosy hay. From the space around him he could tell he was in his carrier rather than the roomier cage in Billy's bedroom. Harry often slept in the carrier when Billy wanted him close at meal times, or when he did homework. The carrier sat on the kitchen table so the two friends could be next to each other.

Harry stretched out his front paws and yawned. *Oh, that was a good sleep*, he thought. For some reason, the hay felt finer than usual. It smelled sweeter too. He took a nibble. *Mmmm, delicious!* Harry sighed happily and tucked into more strands of hay. No doubt it tasted extra-good because Monty had cleared off. *He might look like me*, thought Harry, *but we're* VERY *different*.

Harry finished a particularly tasty strand of hay and looked for his nugget bowl. That was strange – it wasn't where he remembered. Usually it lived by the door of the carrier. Now it was on the far side. And, come to think of it, it was a completely different bowl. Billy must have bought him a new one – that was kind! Instead of orange plastic, the new bowl was made of fine white china. It even had a little crest on it. Harry admired the bowl for a moment. It did look smart, although he'd loved his plastic bowl almost as much as he loved the nuggets inside it.

Thoughts of nuggets made Harry's belly rumble, so he toddled over to scoff a few. As he passed the door of the carrier he glanced outside. *Hang on*. That didn't look like the Smiths' kitchen. Harry stared at the view, puzzled. It didn't look like

Billy's bedroom either, or any of the rooms in the Smiths' flat. Nor did it look like the inside of Mr Smith's van. So, where was he?

Harry considered this for a moment, but then an amazing smell wafted from the bowl. *Mmmm! What was that?* He hurried over and took a look. Inside the bowl was a pile of nuggets, for sure, but nothing like the ones Harry was used to. They looked and smelled wonderful, and a hasty guzzle confirmed that, yes, they tasted wonderful too. Oh, those nuggets were good! Billy must have gone to the pet shop and found a new brand. *You're the best*, thought Harry.

As Harry closed his eyes in bliss, he felt something very strange. The carrier appeared to be . . . moving. In fact, everything around the carrier seemed to be moving too! Harry felt a flash of fear. *Yikes*, he thought. *What's happening?* His mind raced through the possibilities: stolen by burglars, kidnapped by pet-nappers, abducted by aliens . . .

A familiar voice broke into his thoughts.

'Nearly there, Alfie,' it said. 'Put your screen away. We need to get Monty cleaned up as soon as we get there.'

UNCLE KEVIN?

Harry looked around in panic as the truth hit him like a ton of nuggets. Suddenly it all made sense – the fragrant hay, the china bowl, the luxury food. *They think I'm Monty!* he thought. *I'm in their car on the way to the television centre. Oh my goodness, what am I going to do?*

Harry was about to **WHEEK** for help when he spotted a scattering of spinach leaves hidden in the hay. If there was one thing certain to calm Harry down (apart from Billy, of course), it was spinach. Harry gobbled a particularly green-looking leaf. **YUM!** Just like everything else belonging to Monty, that leaf was special. *Monty certainly enjoys the finer things in life*, thought Harry as he guzzled another leaf, then another and another. *Maybe being 'Monty' for a while won't be so bad after all. I think I'll give it a try!*

CHAPTER 6

You're a star, Harry Stevenson!

As Harry Stevenson polished off the last of the spinach leaves, he realized that Uncle Kevin and Auntie Jen's car had come to a stop. The car doors opened smoothly as everyone got out. It was very different from Mr Smith's van, which creaked and squeaked. Harry hunkered down in the luxury hay as Alfie picked up the carrier. He didn't want to be discovered just yet – there might be more of Monty's food coming his way! Uncle Kevin clicked what looked like a tiny remote control at the car, and there was an expensive-sounding *clunk* as the doors locked. *Wow, that's snazzy,* thought Harry Stevenson. *I like being part of this family.* He peered from the carrier as the family walked past a line of other big shiny cars, towards the shiny entrance of the shiny TV station building. *This is just what I thought TV would be like,* thought Harry. *Everything is so sparkly.*

And it wasn't just the building that was shiny and sparkly – the people in it were too! From the uniformed guards who held the doors open when they saw Alfie and Monty, to the smiling staff on reception, everyone looked good. Even the people who rushed around with clipboards did it in a stylish way. It was like they'd just brushed their hair, put on their smartest clothes and smiled for a flattering photograph. It was all very different from life at home. There were no lost socks or scuffed shoes here, thought Harry. He looked down at his dirty paws and wiped them on the hay. He wanted to look shiny too.

The family waited in the building's reception area – a big, airy space with a buzzy feel. Harry gazed around and took in the view. It was fun to feel part of the showbiz world. In fact, it was so fun that he forgot why he was there. It was only when a woman wearing a *Super-Pets* T-shirt and an extra-big smile came over that Harry remembered. The feeling of panic returned, but the woman seemed so thrilled to meet 'Monty' that Harry relaxed. *I am a star!* he thought. *Or at least, everyone thinks I am. I may as well enjoy it.*

'Alfie, Monty!' beamed the woman. 'My name's Tiffany and I'm a big, BIG fan! It's so good to see you – welcome!'

Tiffany peered inside the carrier. Her smile faltered a little and she took a step back in surprise. Harry was still very dusty!

'I see Monty's a little travel-worn,' said Tiffany. 'Come on, let's get him into Make-Up. We need him looking his best for TV.'

OOOOOOOOHHHHH, thought Harry Stevenson. *They're going to make me shiny!*

Tiffany led them down long corridors bustling with activity. There were people carrying cameras and lights, caterers pushing trolleys of delicious-looking food, and actors wearing all sorts of costumes. Harry stared wide-eyed as a group of pirates hurried along, then some acrobats tumbled past. It was all very confusing.

Next, Harry's group passed a line of doors with silver stars on them. Below each star was the name of an actor or TV presenter. Alfie read them out excitedly, and Harry recognized lots from the Smiths' favourite shows.

'It could be your name there one day, Alfie,' said Uncle Kevin.

'And Monty's too!' replied Alfie. 'Monty' purred with pride. Harry was really enjoying his day as someone else! He imagined a life in showbusiness: it would mean he could eat luxury nuggets three times a day, laze around on the finest hay and people would hold doors open for him. That *never* happened at home.

The last door didn't have a person's name on it. Instead, it said:

3

Hair and
Make-Up

'Are you ready for some showbiz magic, everyone?' asked Tiffany as she opened the door.

Ooh, yes, please! thought Harry Stevenson.

CHAPTER 7

Time to Shine,
Harry Stevenson

Harry Stevenson blinked as the door opened and a rush of noise and chatter spilled out.

'TA-DA!' said Tiffany, giving a little bow and welcoming the family inside.

Harry looked around. He could see a hall full of tables, each topped with a mirror that was framed with lights. On every table stood

a pet being prepared for the show by a team of groomers. Everyone was working hard to get the pets looking their best – but they all stopped to stare when the new contestants arrived. Harry could feel the gaze of humans and animals on his carrier as the family made their way across the room. He shrank down in the hay and peeped out shyly. He could see all sorts of pets – dogs, cats, mice, a parrot or two, even a goat!

'Here we are!' said Tiffany finally. 'This is Zane, he's a total darling and he'll take good care of you.'

Harry stared at Zane from top to toe. There was a lot to take in: chunky silver trainers, zebra-striped jeans, a jazzily printed shirt and a giant gold necklace, all topped off with a spiky mane of hair AND mirrored sunglasses. *If anyone can make me shiny, Zane can*, thought Harry, impressed.

'Let's have a look at our little star,' said Zane, and Harry gulped as Alfie placed him on the table. A small cloud of dust arose from Harry's fur and everyone coughed. Harry cringed. He noticed that even Alfie's hands were dusty from holding him.

'Hmmm,' frowned Zane. 'Well, I like a challenge, and you're certainly that, Monty.' He rolled up his sleeves and picked up a comb. 'Let's get to work.'

Harry Stevenson had had baths before and wasn't too keen – but this time was different. Zane was a master at making people (and guinea pigs) feel relaxed and pampered. He knew the loveliest way to massage shampoo into dusty fur, the perfect temperature for water and the ideal amount of bubbles. Harry wallowed happily in the warm soapy bath, while everyone fussed over him. *This is the life*, he thought!

It took several sink-loads of water to wash the grime from Harry's fur, but now he was cleaner and sweeter smelling than ever before. Harry purred with bliss as Zane gently patted him dry with a warm, heated towel. His fur was so fluffy that it puffed out into a soft ginger cloud. Then Zane combed out Harry's whiskers and even gave his teeth a brush!

Harry stared into the mirror. A handsome, well-groomed guinea pig with sparkly eyes looked back. *Is that really me?* thought Harry. *I am gorgeous!*

'Fabulous,' sighed Zane, tired after all his work. Even his spiky mane had sagged a bit. 'You look like a star again, Monty. Just one more thing, let's give those nails a trim. Can you hold him for me, Alfie?'

But – oh dear. Nobody knew quite how much Harry HATED having his nails cut! As Zane advanced with the clippers, Harry panicked. He wriggled and jiggled in Alfie's hands, leaped out of his grasp, through the air . . . and landed in a bowl of dirty water!

WHOOSH!!!!!!!!!

For a small guinea pig, Harry made a surprisingly large splash. The filthy water went up, up, up . . . and back down on to the pets that were being groomed. **SPLOSH!** They didn't look so shiny now!

The wet animals fled in all directions, shaking water everywhere. The floor got slippy and several owners fell as they chased their pets. The goat got overexcited and started to headbutt the groomers. OUCH! It was chaos!

When everyone calmed down, and Auntie Jen had said sorry for what seemed like the hundredth time, Harry let himself be washed, dried and brushed – all over again. Zane didn't seem quite so relaxed this time.

'Monty!' scolded Alfie. 'You're really not yourself today.'

CHAPTER 8

Pawfect,
Harry Stevenson

The primping and fussing went on . . . and on
. . . and on. Harry Stevenson started to feel
bored. *Surely I look sparkly enough now*, he
thought. But, no, Harry's whiskers had to
be waxed, and his claws polished until they
shone. Harry stopped wishing he was Monty,
and started to pine for his quiet, normal life

with Billy. Normal life would have to hang on for a bit, though, because now it was time for Alfie and 'Monty' to head to the Green Room, a kind of waiting room for the show.

'Good luck, the pair of you,' said Auntie Jen, giving Alfie a hug and 'Monty' a nose scratch. 'We'll be watching you in the ring and cheering you on.'

'You can do it, Alfie!' said Uncle Kevin proudly. 'Go for it!'

Harry noticed that Auntie Jen and Uncle Kevin looked a little nervous as they waved goodbye. *I wonder why?* he thought. Then he remembered how difficult Alfie and Monty's tricks were. They were going to have to perform them on live TV soon, and Monty wasn't here yet. He wouldn't have much time to prepare when he got here! Harry started to feel worried for Alfie and Monty.

It's all right, he thought. Billy and the Smiths must have noticed he was missing by now. *Yes, Billy would definitely be able to tell the difference. He'll be here soon,* Harry told himself. *Then everything will be sorted and Monty can do his tricks.*

Disappointingly for Harry Stevenson, the Green Room was not full of spinach, and there didn't seem to be any lettuce in there either. Instead the *Super-Pets* judges were mingling with all the contestants. Harry watched from a comfy sofa. He recognized the judges from TV, and he was so excited to be in the same room that he forgot to be worried. Harry nearly **wheeked** out loud when he saw Mrs Smith's favourite judge. She always said how handsome the judge was, but on seeing him close up, Harry had to disagree. For some reason, the man's face was as orange as Harry!

'Look, Monty!' breathed Alfie. 'It's Madam Poppy and her Pawfect Pups . . . and she's coming our way!'

Harry followed Alfie's gaze and spied a jolly-looking lady wearing a pink top hat and tailcoat over a fussy blouse and tartan slacks. She was walking around the Green

Room, surrounded by what seemed to be a blizzard of snowy white fur. Harry looked closer and saw that the blizzard was in fact six little dogs – tiny, fluffy things with pink button noses and tails like pom-poms.

Madam Poppy had dressed each dog in a matching pink cape and bow tie. A crowd gathered around her, *oohing* and *aahing*.

Then, suddenly, Harry heard a snarl and a cry of surprise! One man, thinking that the dogs were cute, had bent down to stroke some fluffy fur. It wasn't a good idea. *Oh dear,* thought Harry Stevenson, as the man stepped away hastily. The dog was giving him a steely look that could *never* be called cute.

'They're not pets, you know!' trilled Madam Poppy. 'My little darlings are showbiz professionals. Best to look but don't touch!'

'The Pawfect Pups won *Super-Pets* last year,' whispered Alfie. 'They're the ones to beat.'

It looked like Madam Poppy was taking no chances when it came to keeping her winning title: Harry could see that she was going round the room to check out the other competitors.

'What a sweet little act,' she cooed when she got to Alfie and Harry. 'It's wonderful to see amateurs having a go.'

Harry didn't know what 'amateur' meant, but from the way the dogs were looking at him he guessed it wasn't very flattering.

'Just ignore them, Monty,' whispered Alfie when Madam Poppy and the pups had passed. 'We'll show them, won't we?'

But Harry wasn't listening. He'd found that the pot plants in the Green Room were very tasty indeed.

CHAPTER 9

Get ready,
Harry Stevenson

Finally, *Super-Pets* was on air! A ginormous screen in the Green Room flickered into life and started showing the programme as it was filmed in the studio next door. Harry heard its familiar theme tune and looked up to see the show's presenter bound onstage.

'Ladies and gentlemen,' cried the presenter, 'boys and girls, birdies and beasties – are you ready? It's time forrrrr . . .'

'SUPER-PETS!' yelled the audience.

The judges wished everyone luck and headed through the door that led from the Green Room to the TV studio. Shortly after, they appeared on the screen! Harry was entranced. It was like magic! He was so amazed to see the show happening in real life that he forgot to be worried for Alfie and Monty.

The first contestants were called from the Green Room. Harry watched them vanish through the door, then reappear on the TV screen. He settled down to enjoy the show.

'And here we have Captain Jeff and his Singing Rat,' said the presenter. Harry marvelled as the rat sat on Captain Jeff's flat cap and squeaked out the tune to 'Greensleeves'.

'Wonderful stuff,' gushed the presenter. 'That rat can certainly hold a tune! But is it enough to win tonight's big prize? Remember, there's a year's supply of luxury pet food at stake, as well as that all-important title.'

Next it was the turn of Farmer Jane and Gloria the Pig. They put on a dazzling tap-dance routine that left the audience open-mouthed with amazement. Gloria was a talented pig, to be sure. The presenter loved the dance so much she could hardly find words to describe it. In the end she called it 'eye-popping' and 'unforgettable'. Harry had to agree.

On went the show. As this was the series finale, all the performances were excellent. The goat had a football kickabout with its owner, a parrot read poetry, a cockatoo told hilarious jokes and a cat played the violin with its teeth!

This is the best episode yet, thought Harry Stevenson happily.

Then it was time for Madam Poppy.

'Now, folks, what you've all been waiting for,' said the presenter. 'Here are last year's FABULOUS winners, back with their awesome obstacle course – or should that be pawsome? Ladies and gentlemen, I give you, Madam Poppy and her Pawfect Pups!!'

'Good luck,' said Alfie as Madam Poppy

and the pups left the Green Room. She gave a syrupy smile. 'Us professionals don't need *luck*, dear,' she said. 'You keep it for yourself and your little orange hamster.'

Harry looked around to see where the hamster was, but he couldn't spot it.

Thunderous applause filled the studio as Madam Poppy strode into the arena, followed by her procession of cape-wearing fluffies. The dogs pranced along with dainty steps, snooty noses held high in the air.

'SIIIIIIIITTTT,' screeched Madam Poppy – and six furry bottoms dropped to the floor. Madam Poppy gave a flashy bow to the audience and the Pawfect Pups did the same, touching the ground with their noses.

'Awwwww,' cooed the crowd.

Madam Poppy set off around the obstacle course, followed by the pups running nose to tail in perfect formation. Everyone cheered as the little dogs whizzed around the course. Their fluffy white tails and silky pink capes flew behind them as they sped along, jumping over hurdles, leaping through hoops and weaving through slalom poles with ease.

At the end of the course, Madam Poppy and the dogs stood in a dead-straight row.

Then, as Madam Poppy stepped forward and made a deep bow, three of the Pawfect Pups lined up next to her. Two more dogs scrambled on top of them, and finally the very last pup climbed on *them* to form a white, fluffy doggy tower. The dog at the top stood on its hind legs and lifted one of its front paws to wave to the crowd, who went wild!

That was really special, thought Harry.

'MAGNIFICENT,' said the presenter. 'WHAT A SHOW! It's going to take something very special indeed to beat *that*.'

'We can do it, Monty!' hissed Alfie.

We can do what? thought Harry, his attention focused on the pups.

And then, in a horrible rush, he realized

what Alfie meant. YIKES!

Harry looked wildly around the Green Room, hoping against hope that Billy would appear with Monty. But what he saw instead filled him with terror. He'd been so wrapped up in watching the show that he hadn't noticed the room emptying behind him. Now he and Alfie were the only contestants left. So that must mean . . . they were on next!

I can't do tricks, panicked Harry. *I'll be hopeless, and it'll be on live TV too. Somebody, quickly, stop the show! I don't want to be Monty any more!*

But it looked like he'd have to!

It was SHOWTIME.

CHAPTER 10

Showtime,
Harry Stevenson!

'And now we have our final contestants,' called the presenter. 'Ladies and gentlemen, please give a warm welcome to our youngest stars, Alfie and Monty!'

Harry Stevenson shook with fright as Alfie picked him up from the sofa and headed from the Green Room into the TV studio. He shook even more when Alfie walked onstage. It was hot and bright there, from all the lights and cameras. Behind the stage was a huge screen, ten times as big as the one in the Green Room. Harry looked up and gulped. His giant, scared face was beaming out to the audience in the studio and everyone watching at home. The Harry on-screen looked remarkably 'shiny' – but Harry didn't care about that now. He just wanted to be back to normal; scruffy and snug at home.

Harry could see that the TV studio was **ENORMOUS!** To him, it felt as big as the Sparky FC football stadium. The arena in front of the stage was still set up with the

Pawfect Pups' obstacle course, and the rows and rows of seats around it were packed with people. Harry desperately scanned the rows for a familiar face. *Where are you, Billy?* he thought. *I can't do this. Please come and rescue me!*

But Billy was nowhere to be seen.

'Alfie, Monty,' beamed the presenter, holding a microphone to Alfie. 'How are you feeling about tonight?'

'We're feeling pretty good, thanks!' beamed Alfie.

'And what about Monty?' joked the presenter, leaning down to Harry.

Harry seized his chance and sounded the emergency klaxon.

'WHEEK, WHEEK, WHEEEK! WHEEK, WHEEK, WHEEEK!' he cried into the microphone.

If you were a guinea pig, you'd know that this meant: *THERE'S BEEN A MIX-UP, GET ME OUT OF HERE!*

But instead of thinking 'Monty' was

unhappy, Alfie started to giggle.

'Monty's excited,' he said, smiling. 'He can't wait to do his tricks on TV.'

'That guinea pig's a born performer!' chuckled the presenter. 'Aren't you, Monty?'

'I'M NOT MONTY, I'M HARRY, AND I WANT TO GO HOME, PLEASE!' cried Harry – but all the humans heard was, **'WHEEK, WHEEK, WHEEK!'**

To Harry's dismay, everyone in the audience started to laugh too. *Oh dear,* thought Harry Stevenson. *Oh dear, oh dear, oh dear!*

'My goodness, he's keen!' cried the presenter. 'I can't *wait* to see what Monty's got in store for us tonight! Nor can our viewers, I bet – and there are millions and millions of them!'

Millions and millions? thought Harry. Things were getting worse!

By now the stage was ready for Alfie and 'Monty', and all their props had been laid out. The crowd hushed as Alfie placed Harry on the floor. It was time to begin their routine. Harry could hear his heart thumping like mad. He looked down and saw that his paws were trembling. He was terrified!

'OK, Monty,' whispered Alfie. 'Just do what we practised.'

Harry tried his best, he really did. He managed a wobbly high-five, which brought cheers from the crowd, but spinning wasn't as easy as it looked – walking in a circle made Harry dizzy and he wobbled off in a zig-zaggy line! After that, *everything* went wrong. Harry tried to remember what Monty had done for each trick, but he kept getting muddled. He broke the bangle on Alfie's wrist, knocked over the hurdles and dropped the ball every time he tried to pick it up.

'You can do it, Monty, I know you can,' coaxed Alfie desperately. But Harry couldn't.

A dreadful silence fell across the studio.

'Come on, Monty!' called a person kindly, and soon everyone had joined in.

'MON-TY.' 'MON-TY.' 'MON-TY.'

It was no good. In the end, Harry felt so awful that he crept into the tunnel and refused to move! Alfie called and called, but Harry wouldn't budge. *No one can see me in here*, he thought. *And that's how I like it. Showbiz and shininess is not for me!* Harry could see Alfie's worried face peering into the end of the tunnel, and he heard the presenter walking over.

'Never mind, Alfie,' she said kindly. 'You've done really well to get this far. Come on, it's time for the judging.'

'You're not Monty, are you?' sighed Alfie as he reached inside the tunnel. 'You're just Harry Stevenson.'

CHAPTER 11

Go, go, go, Harry Stevenson!

This is the worst moment of my life, thought Harry Stevenson, as Alfie picked him up, tucked him under his arm and trudged out of the spotlight. The crowd felt so sorry for the pair that everyone clapped. It didn't make Harry feel any happier, though, and Alfie looked like he was going to cry.

All the other competitors were waiting in a special area at the ringside. Harry could see the Pawfect Pups staring at him scornfully. Madam Poppy was smirking, no doubt thinking that she'd won, and even the goat was looking smug. But as Alfie started the sad walk to join them, there was a faint cry from across the studio.

Harry jerked his head up. Was that who he thought it was?

'Harry!' came the cry again.

'WHEEK, WHEEK, WHEEK!' called Harry in reply. **'WHEEK, WHEEK, WHEEK!'**

Billy's here!!!

Harry peered out from the spotlights, looking for the face he loved best. At last! There was Billy, on the far side of the room. Harry wriggled out of Alfie's hands and jumped on to the floor. He was desperate to see his friend again! Harry raced towards Billy, but his route took him right through the Pawfect Pups' obstacle course.

As Harry made his way across the course the audience started to notice his progress. Soon they were pointing and shouting and cheering! You see, Harry was so eager to get to Billy that he was doing a perfect round of the obstacle course. He was speeding along in record time, acing every obstacle in front of him!

'Well, this IS a turn-up for the books,' gasped the presenter, as the TV cameras zoomed in on Harry Stevenson. 'Who'd have thought that a plucky little guinea pig could run so fast or jump so high?'

The crowd roared their encouragement to Harry, rising to their feet to get a better view. Spotlights followed as he whizzed through the tunnels, soared over jumps, scampered round the slalom and then dashed up, along and down the seesaw. His longing to

see Billy again made him amazingly speedy and agile!

I've nearly reached Billy, thought Harry as he flew over the last hurdle in a ginger blur of joy. He was so happy that he did a spectacular series of popcorns that had the crowd raising the roof with their cheers!

BOING, BOING, BOING,

went Harry Stevenson.

'HURRAY!' yelled the crowd.

'AMAZING!' cried the presenter. 'Can you believe your eyes?! I think we've just seen a world record being smashed. Even the speediest dog hasn't got round that course so fast!'

'It's *certainly* a turn-up for the books,' said the head judge. 'It looks like Monty was just waiting for a bigger course to match his talent. That was without a doubt the performance of the evening! Ladies and gentlemen, I think we've found our winner!'

The cameras showed a close-up of the Pawfect Pups. They didn't look quite so smug now. Madam Poppy was scowling horribly.

But Harry didn't notice – he only had eyes for his best friend, Billy Smith. Billy was cuddling him and kissing his ginger furry nose, and Harry was nuzzling his friend in return.

This is the BEST *moment of my life,* thought Harry happily. Because as if being cuddled by Billy wasn't wonderful enough – he also had the prospect of a year's supply of luxury guinea pig food to consider.

CHAPTER 12

Nice trick,
Harry Stevenson

Harry was glad to get back to the Smiths' flat that evening. It had been quite a day. He and Billy had won *Super-Pets* – but because no one could tell them apart, Billy said Alfie and Monty could go onstage to collect their award. It was what they'd been training for, after all. In return, Alfie had offered Harry

the year's supply of pet food, so everyone was happy.

Now all the family was in the living room – Harry and the Smiths, as well as Alfie and Monty, Auntie Jen and Uncle Kevin. Billy (who'd cheered up massively since Harry had wowed the crowd) was telling everyone how he'd spotted the mix-up. He'd offered 'Harry' a pile of carrots, he said, and 'Harry' had refused to eat them. The same thing happened with spinach, beetroot and nuggets.

'There's no way Harry would turn down any kind of guinea pig food,' smiled Billy. 'So I knew it couldn't be him!'

After Billy realized what had happened, the Smiths had piled into the van, taking Monty with them, and raced across town. Harry wondered what Monty had made of travelling in the van. *A taste of normal life will have done him good*, he thought, and Monty was certainly acting less superior after Harry's record-breaking performance. Mr Smith had hoped to reach the TV centre before the show started, but at least they'd got there before it finished and saved the day! Uncle Kevin was so grateful that he'd stopped teasing Billy about his 'ginger rat' and looked at Harry with a new respect.

Alfie and Monty were teaching Billy and Harry how to do tricks. It had taken a few goes, but Harry was starting to get the hang of the 'spin'. Actually, he'd figured out how to do it fairly quickly, but he was pretending not to know so he'd get more nuggets.

'Your guinea pig's pretty cool,' said Alfie. 'The way he ran was amazing!'

'Monty's OK too,' smiled Billy.

The two boys grinned at each other over Monty, who was performing a flashy handstand of sorts.

Huh, thought Harry Stevenson. *Think that's special? I can do* MAGIC! *Just watch – I shall make those spinach leaves disappear.*

And so he did!

STORY 2
Happy holidays,
Harry Stevenson!

CHAPTER 1

Bonjour,
Harry Stevenson

Harry Stevenson was on his way to Paris. Jetsetting travel was unusual for a guinea pig, but Harry Stevenson wasn't your usual kind of guinea pig. For despite Harry's best efforts to live a quiet life, his greedy tummy was always getting him into adventures.

This time, though, Harry's stomach

wasn't to blame. He was travelling to France with his best friend and owner, Billy Smith, and Billy's mum and dad. The Smiths had won a holiday to Paris – and not just any old holiday either! It was a special Christmas break: three nights in a smart hotel with travel and spending money thrown in. Now the family were whizzing towards the airport in Mr Smith's van.

Mrs Smith was very excited because she'd always wanted to see Paris and visit a Christmas market. Harry thought that

Mr Smith was surprisingly keen too – he normally just wanted to stay at home with the family, busy doing jobs or watching his beloved football team, Sparky FC. As for Billy, he hadn't liked the idea at all. Harry had heard a lot about it over the last few days: Christmas wouldn't be the same if they were away from home, fretted Billy. But Harry suspected the real reason was that Billy had never been on an aeroplane before and was feeling nervous.

Billy will be all right with me to look after him, thought Harry Stevenson. *Christmas will be just as nice in Paris, and hopefully there'll be plenty to eat.* Harry always enjoyed Christmas. Billy didn't have to go to school and Mr and Mrs Smith had time off work. That meant all the Smiths were around and Harry got extra attention. Even better, Christmas involved a lot of eating, which was one of Harry's favourite pastimes. Mr and Mrs Smith chopped up mountains of vegetables for their Christmas meals, and quite a few of them ended up in Harry's food bowl. Harry daydreamed about his bowl for a while, before turning his attention back to the Smiths.

Mrs Smith was reading from a guidebook about Paris. It described grand buildings, wide tree-lined streets, pretty parks, a famous tower and wonderful food.

'I know someone who likes good food,' laughed Mr Smith. 'Harry Stevenson would be a big fan of France!'

Harry shrank down guiltily in his hiding place.

Oh, hadn't I mentioned that Harry Stevenson was hiding? Well, he was! Harry was keeping a very low profile in Billy's bag. That's because he wasn't meant to be in the van. As far as Mr and Mrs Smith knew, Harry was tucked up safely in his cage at home! The Smiths' next-door-neighbour Maya Matthews was going to drop by twice a day to top up Harry's food, water and hay. It had all been arranged for weeks.

Harry thought back to that morning, when his unexpected trip began. Mr and Mrs Smith had just left the flat, when Billy dashed back to say goodbye – again. Harry knew his friend was worried about flying, so he'd got ready to give Billy a comforting nuzzle. But to his surprise, Billy had opened his rucksack and tipped most of his clothes on to the floor. Then he'd lifted Harry out of the cage and popped him in the bag!

Harry had squeaked in protest, but Billy put his fingers to his lips and Harry understood that he needed to be quiet. So he'd watched silently as his friend grabbed carrots, nuggets and a bowl, stashing them in his roomy coat pockets. Then Billy had hurried out of the flat to catch up with his parents, carrying Harry Stevenson in the bag. Harry wasn't used to spending the weekend in a rucksack, and he didn't know what travelling by plane would be like, but as long as he was with Billy then everything would be fine.

And even better, thought Harry happily, *we're off on an adventure together. Hurray!*

CHAPTER 2

Red alert,
Harry Stevenson!

Harry Stevenson had never been to an airport before so he was very curious when they got there. He peered out from under the top of the rucksack and sniffed the air. There was a feeling of excitement in the building, which was hard not to share. People were rushing around with suitcases, and looking at screens showing long lists of place names. Harry jumped as a loud voice announced a flight to a place he'd never heard of. He looked around, wondering who'd spoken, but the voice seemed to have come from nowhere.

Travelling is very interesting, thought Harry. Billy had shown Harry where Paris was in his book of maps. It didn't seem that far away on the map – only a few paw lengths. Then he'd pointed to South America, where Harry knew that guinea pigs came from. *South America must be furtherer away than Paris*, thought Harry. It looked much more than ten paw lengths from the Smiths' city. Harry wondered about the first guinea pigs to make that long trip. *I am following in their paw steps*, he thought proudly.

There seemed to be a lot of queueing in airports. First the Smiths had to queue to show their tickets, and then they joined a long line of people waiting to go through 'Security'. Harry wondered what that was. His little eyes peeped out from the bag, but he couldn't see anything apart from the other people queueing.

Finally the Smiths reached the front of the line. A woman in uniform beckoned them forward.

'Everyone, put your bags and coats in a tray and get ready to be scanned,' she said.

'Here we go, Billy,' said Mrs Smith, pointing to a tray. 'Put your things in there, then stay close to me.'

OOH, thought Harry. From his hiding place in the bag he could see a line of trays moving slowly along a conveyor belt. *Am I going on that? It looks fun!*

Sure enough, Billy placed the bag in one of the trays.

'Stay hidden, Harry,' he whispered.

Harry Stevenson got ready to enjoy the ride. *I like airports*, thought Harry, as the tray glided along. It was like being on a slow and gentle rollercoaster. Peeping out, he could see that his tray had reached a sort of plastic tunnel. *I wonder what that does?* thought Harry as the tray neared the tunnel's entrance.

He soon found out.

CLANG, CLANG, CLANG!!!

An awful noise rang out and red lights flashed as Harry's tray passed under the scanner. Harry's fur puffed out in panic as he heard shouts and running footsteps. People were saying things like, 'unexpected item', 'security alert' and 'CODE RED'. Harry wondered why. The tray passed out from the scanner, slid down a chute and came to a stop. **BUMP!**

'It's that bag,' said a voice. 'Be careful, everyone – there could be something dangerous inside.'

Dangerous? thought Harry Stevenson. *That doesn't sound good!* He decided to hide from the danger, whatever it was, and burrowed under Billy's clothes.

As Harry wriggled under a woolly jumper, he heard the sound of a zip opening. Light flooded into Billy's rucksack. *Oh, no, they're looking for the danger in HERE*, trembled Harry. *I hope it's not in the bag with me!* He watched as gloved hands rummaged in the bag. One by one, Billy's clothes were lifted out. Soon there would be no place to hide! Finally, only Harry and the jumper remained. *But where is the danger?* thought Harry. The gloved hand carefully picked up the jumper, then a torch shone into the bag's darkest corners. Harry cowered at the back, blinking in the bright light. Beyond it, Harry could see the faces of people in uniform. The faces looked surprised.

'Well, I never,' said one of them. 'It's a guinea pig!'

'I've seen all sorts here,' said another of the security guards. 'But this takes the biscuit.'

The man turned to Mr and Mrs Smith.

'Sir, madam: do you know this guinea pig?' he asked sternly.

There were very big sighs from Billy's parents.

'I'm afraid we do,' said Mrs Smith. 'BILLY, COME HERE!!!!!'

CHAPTER 3

Let's go,
Harry Stevenson

Harry Stevenson watched from Billy's arms as the Smiths were led out of the airport by a security guard. Everyone stared at Harry. Some people pointed and laughed; a few took photographs. Billy's cheeks were burning with shame and Mr and Mrs Smith looked very, *very* cross. Harry gulped. True,

it wasn't his fault this time – but he still felt awful. Billy was in trouble, and now the Smiths had lost their trip to Paris. There was no way around it: Harry wasn't allowed on the plane, so they'd had to miss their flight.

The walk to the car park seemed to take ages. No one spoke. As the Smiths reached the van, a plane passed noisily overhead. It had just taken off and was heading somewhere exciting – Paris, maybe. Mrs Smith sighed, and Billy hung his head.

'I'm REALLY sorry, Mum and Dad,' he said.

Harry expected a huge row, but it never came. Instead, Mr Smith shrugged and ruffled Billy's hair.

'Billy, I don't know WHAT you were thinking in bringing Harry, but . . . what's done is done. Come on, we can still make this work. Let's DRIVE to Paris. I feel like a road trip!'

Billy's eyes widened. 'Are you sure, Dad?' he squeaked.

Mrs Smith *wasn't* sure, as it was a long way – but Mr Smith kept on. It would be an adventure, he said. A Christmas to always remember: just the four of them, the van, and Paris.

That means I'm going too, thought Harry, and his heart leaped. He **WHEEK-WHEEKED** with excitement.

Mrs Smith laughed.

'Oh, all right, then,' she said. 'It's mad but it would be a shame to miss Paris. I haven't had an adventure for years.'

So it was decided. Mr and Mrs Smith looked at their phones to find the best way

to Paris. The trains were all booked, but there were still spaces on the ferry. Guinea pigs were allowed on ferries, it seemed.

'Right,' said Mr Smith. 'Let's head to the port!'

Harry didn't have to hide now, so he snuggled up on Billy's lap as the van sped away. Mr Smith put on his favourite music and he and Mrs Smith sang along. Billy cringed, but Harry tapped his paws cheerfully. He loved it when the Smiths were happy.

Paris, here we come! thought Harry.

An hour later, the Smiths were not quite so happy. In fact, they were all rather cross.

Not long into the journey, Mr Smith's van had started to make alarming noises. Then came a funny smell that had made Billy hold his nose. The van had jerked on for a few more minutes, but had finally spluttered and banged to a halt.

Now they were waiting in a layby beside the road to the port. A mechanic had come in a truck to mend the van, but things weren't looking good.

'I can fix the problem,' said the mechanic, 'but I'll have to do it back at the garage. I need to order the parts so it'll take a day or so.'

Oh, no! thought Harry, looking at the Smiths' downcast faces. *We'll never get to Paris now.*

The mechanic offered the Smiths a lift back to the city.

'Come on, let's go home,' sighed Mrs Smith. 'I thought this trip was too good to be true.'

But Mr Smith didn't want to give up just yet.

'Hang on for five minutes,' he said to the mechanic.

Mr Smith seemed determined to get to Paris. *He really must want to see the Christmas markets*, thought Harry, as he watched Mr Smith pacing around the layby, trying to think of a solution.

Five minutes passed but Mr Smith was still pacing. When *fifteen* minutes had gone by, Mrs Smith marched over to him. She and Mr Smith 'had words', as they called it. The words sounded angry to Harry. There was a lot of hand-waving and stomping about too. It went on for ages, and they didn't notice the mechanic starting his truck.

'I've got to head off now,' he called out of the window. 'Are you coming?'

'Mum! Dad!' yelled Billy. 'We need to go!'

But Mr and Mrs Smith didn't hear over the noise of the traffic. The mechanic called again – still no reply. So he shrugged his shoulders and drove the truck away, towing the van behind.

Harry watched from Billy's arms as the truck and van sped off.

EVERYTHING'S going wrong today, he thought.

CHAPTER 4

Born to be wild,
Harry Stevenson?

As Harry Stevenson stared after the van, he
noticed that the traffic was slowing down.
Perhaps there were workmen digging up the
road further on. Soon the traffic crawled
to a halt. In among the cars and lorries
was a huge, noisy motorbike, ridden by
an enormous biker. Harry spotted another

biker, and another. There were about twenty of them, all looking mean and scary.

'Erm, Harry, I think that biker's staring at us,' muttered Billy.

Harry looked at the first biker. Sure enough, the man's eyes were fixed on Billy – or, more particularly, Harry Stevenson. Harry shrank down in fear. *Why is that man looking at me?* Harry fretted. He was scared by the biker's fierce-looking face and big bushy beard.

Still staring at Harry, the biker revved his engine. **BRMM, BRMMM!** Then all the other bikers did too. **BRMM, BRMM, BRMMM!** What a noise! Harry gave a chirrup of fright. Billy edged back towards his parents, who were still 'having words'. Harry felt safer next to Mr and Mrs Smith.

But the lead biker turned his bike towards the Smiths and drove into the layby! The others followed, coming to a halt in a circle around the Smiths. Mr and Mrs Smith stopped their row and looked up in surprise.

What's going on? wondered Harry. The lead biker stepped off his bike and walked over to the Smiths in his big leather boots:

STOMP, STOMP, STOMP.

The metal chains around the biker's neck jangled as he moved. Harry gulped. The man looked even scarier close up. Underneath his leather jacket, his hands and arms were covered with tattoos.

The biker stood in front of the Smiths and rolled up his sleeve to reveal muscles that would win any arm-wrestling match on the planet. Was he going to arm-wrestle Mr Smith, perhaps? Harry gulped again, and took a closer look at the tattoos. No doubt they were of dragons, or dinosaurs, or, even worse, a snake!

Hang on . . .

Harry peered closer.

Was that . . . a guinea pig?

Harry looked again. Yes, it was. And not just one: all the tattoos were guinea pigs! A whole herd of them danced across the man's beefy biceps. Harry heard Billy and his parents gasp as they spotted them. The man held out his gigantic, guinea-pig-covered hand.

'All right, people? My name's Thor and I'm the leader of this lot,' he growled, gesturing to the bikers behind him. 'We're called *Los Cavies Locos.*'

Harry twitched with surprise. He knew what 'cavy' meant – guinea pig! But why did the bikers have that name? Did they eat cavies for breakfast?

Thor smiled, and all of a sudden he looked cuddly rather than terrifying.

'We spotted your little guinea pig there,' Thor continued. 'It just so happens we've all got a thing about guinea pigs.' The other bikers nodded their heads. 'Had them as kids and never shook the habit. Thought they'd make the perfect mascot for our gang.'

To Harry's horror, Billy held him up to Thor!

'Guinea pigs are the best, aren't they, Thor?' said Billy. 'This is Harry Stevenson. What are yours called?'

Harry looked bravely into Thor's craggy face. The eyes that met his own were kind and twinkly. *PHEW*, thought Harry. *Thor really does love cavies!*

'He looks just like my Gnasher,' sighed Thor, tickling Harry on the nose. 'He was my first guinea pig, back when I was a lad.' Thor proudly pointed to his tattoos. 'That's Gnasher here. And these are Thunder, Chaos, Zombie, and, er . . . Snuggles.'

Now all the members of the gang showed off *their* guinea pig tattoos. Then everyone admired Harry Stevenson, who basked in the gang's approval.

'So,' said Thor. 'It looks like you're in trouble. We can't let a fellow cavy-lover down – what can we do to help?'

The Smiths explained their problem.

'Easy,' said Thor. 'Hop on the back of our bikes and we'll take you to the port. We always carry spare helmets, just in case. Billy and Harry, you come with me. Mum and Dad, you go with Vulcan and Storm.'

'On you get,' Thor said as Mr Smith looked nervously at Vulcan and his bike. 'Or do you prefer this layby to Paris?'

That did it! Harry watched Mr Smith jump on to the back of Vulcan's motorbike. And with a mighty roar of engines, *Los Cavies Locos* took to the road with their new members, the Smiths.

CHAPTER 5

Ahoy there, Harry Stevenson!

Bombing down the motorway with a gang of bikers made life in the hutch seem very tame. Harry Stevenson peeped out of Billy's bag as they zoomed along. His whiskers were pinned backwards by the wind, and his ginger fur was blown into his eyes. Harry wished he had a pair of goggles, like Thor's.

Some earmuffs might be useful too. The bike's engine growled, the wind howled, and cars and lorries thundered alongside them. Every now and again, Vulcan and Storm's bikes caught up with Thor's, and Harry could see Mr and Mrs Smith holding on to their bikers for dear life. Mr Smith had his eyes shut with fright the whole time, but Mrs Smith seemed happier. At one point she even winked at Billy. *Well*, thought Harry. *She'd wanted an adventure!*

It didn't take long to reach the port. As *Los Cavies Locos* roared into the car park, scattering tourists and workers, Harry caught a glimpse of the ferry ahead. He blinked and looked up, up and up again. The ferry was as tall as the tower blocks near the Smiths' flat!

Are we really going on that? he wondered, feeling even smaller than usual. Billy seemed awed too.

'We'd better be off,' said Thor, helping Billy and Harry off the bike. 'You can join our gang when you're older, Billy,' he winked. Then he revved his engine, circled around and led the gang out of the port.

'Bye, Thor! Bye, Vulcan! Bye, Storm!' called Billy. 'And thank you!'

'Well, *that* was eventful,' said Mr Smith when the noise of the bikes' engines had faded. 'I must say I did enjoy that ride. I've always fancied myself as a biker.'

Harry saw Mrs Smith and Billy exchange a look. Mr Smith must have seen it too, because he blushed.

'Come on, then,' he said. 'Let's catch that ferry!'

Harry Stevenson had seen some surprising sights in his life, but nothing could prepare him for his first glimpse of the ocean. The Smiths were sitting on a bench on deck, enjoying the view as the ferry sailed to France. Their fellow passengers seemed confused to have a guinea pig among them, but Harry didn't care. He was too busy trying to spot where the sea ended. Harry wrinkled up his sparkly eyes and looked all around, but all he could see was bluey-grey water.

Billy had told Harry about the names for guinea pigs around the world, so

Harry knew that lots of them meant 'little sea pig'. *Now I really AM a little sea pig*, he thought proudly. Harry didn't feel quite such a 'sea pig' when some gulls whizzed alongside the boat. The seagulls stared at him with cold, hungry eyes, so he hid under Billy's coat. *Yikes!*

'We'll be in Paris for tea!' said Mr Smith, drumming his fingers on the rail around the deck. 'Are you excited, Billy? *I* am!'

'I'm glad you're so excited, dear,' smiled Mrs Smith, looking up from her guidebook. 'I never thought you'd be that keen.'

Me neither, thought Harry. *Why does Mr Smith want to go to Paris so much?*

'It's the Christmas markets,' replied Mr Smith. 'I can't wait.'

Just then, Billy stood up and pointed towards the horizon.

'I can see France!' he cried. 'Land ahoy!'

We're nearly there! squeaked Harry Stevenson.

CHAPTER 6

You're in Paris,
Harry Stevenson!

The plan was to catch a train from the port to Paris. But when the Smiths got to the railway station, none of the trains were running because the train drivers were on strike! There was a coach service to Paris instead. So Harry Stevenson and the Smiths had to go to the back of yet another queue.

Everyone waited and waited. Gradually the sky turned darker and it began to get chilly. Harry snuggled inside Billy's coat, fluffing up his fur so he was like a furry hot water bottle, but Billy started to shiver. Mr Smith unzipped his bag, rummaged around and pulled out a scarf. The scarf looked familiar, thought Harry. Ah, yes – it was Mr Smith's Sparky FC scarf, the one he wore to matches.

'I thought I told you not to bring that,' said Mrs Smith. 'You can't walk around an elegant city like Paris in a football scarf!'

'I brought it in case it was cold,' said Mr Smith. 'And it is! Here you go, Billy.'

'Thanks, Dad,' said Billy gratefully as he

wrapped the scarf around him.

Just then, a minibus pulled to a stop, and a cheery man leaned out.

'I recognize that scarf!' he said. 'Need a lift, Sparky fans? We're heading to Paris.'

Harry looked hopefully at Mr and Mrs Smith. They didn't seem too sure, but at that point Billy sneezed.

'We'd love a lift, thanks,' said Mrs Smith. 'It's freezing out here and our son is getting cold.'

'Hop in the back, then, folks,' said the man.

Harry peeped out from a gap in Billy's coat as the Smiths went to the back of the minibus. The door swung open and a

friendly-looking lady
popped her head out.

'Come inside!' she
said. 'You poor things,
you look half-frozen.'

'You've got a Sparky
scarf too!' said Mrs
Smith. 'Are you a
fan?'

'I am indeed,'
smiled the lady.
'We all are!'

As the Smiths
climbed into
the minibus,
Harry saw what

she meant. The minibus was full of people and EVERYONE was wearing a Sparky FC scarf. Some wore Sparky tracksuits, others had Sparky hats, and there were Sparky flags draped across the seats.

Mrs Smith's mouth dropped open in surprise. 'Wow, what a lot of Sparky fans!' she gasped. 'What a coincidence you're going to Paris as well.'

Mr Smith coughed. Harry turned to him and saw he was looking shifty, very shifty indeed.

'We're heading to the big game,' said the lady who'd let them in. 'The Sparks versus PSG. Aren't you going?'

'You didn't mention that Sparky were playing in Paris!' exclaimed Mrs Smith, turning to her husband.

'Erm . . . it must have slipped my mind,' mumbled Mr Smith, who looked shiftier than ever.

'We're going to the Christmas markets,' explained Mrs Smith, with a steely eye on Mr Smith. 'My husband wanted to see them *especially*. Didn't you, dear?'

At last Harry Stevenson and the Smiths reached Paris. What a journey it had been! The last leg in the minibus had been fun, though. The Sparky fans turned out to be lovely people, and were thrilled to discover that a VIP (Very Important Pig) was in their midst. They'd recognized Harry from the time he'd scored a winning goal last season, and when he'd stopped the theft of

Sparky FC's silver trophy. There had been laughing and joking and *lots* of funny football songs. Even Mrs Smith had put down her guidebook and joined in a song or two. All the fans wanted their photo taken with Harry, and they were so happy to meet him that they'd driven the Smiths the whole way to their hotel – and offered them a lift back home too!

The minibus gave a *toot toot* as it headed off, and the Smiths turned towards the hotel. 'Come on,' said Mrs Smith, looking at her watch. 'Let's check in, get some food and have an early night. It's been crazy today and I'm bushed! Then we can get up early and have a full day tomorrow.'

Do we HAVE to go to bed? thought Harry Stevenson. *We're in PARIS!* Harry looked around to see if he could spot anything from Mrs Smith's guidebook, but he was so tired he drifted off to sleep.

CHAPTER 7

Regarde,
Harry Stevenson!

The next morning was brightly lit with cold winter sunshine – the perfect weather for sightseeing, said Mrs Smith. Sightseeing turned out to involve a lot of walking, so Harry Stevenson was glad to be carried in Billy's bag. It would have been hard to keep up, with his little legs. Harry stuck his head out of the bag, taking everything in. Paris was certainly beautiful. The Smiths passed through narrow streets crammed with cafes, and along grand avenues lined with smart-looking shops. Mrs Smith was delighted, pointing out the famous places listed in her guidebook. Well-dressed people stalked by, hurrying to work or play, and in too much of a rush to notice a small ginger guinea pig staring at them. All around was the chatter of people talking, arguing and joking in French. Harry had no idea what they were saying, but it all sounded glamorous and exciting. *How different Paris is from home*, he thought.

The Smiths' walk continued past art galleries, museums and gardens. They stopped in a cafe for pastries and *chocolat chaud* – which Billy said was the nicest hot chocolate he'd ever tasted. Moving on, the Smiths passed a street artist who was drawing portraits of tourists. The Smiths watched for a while, admiring his skill, and then Billy and Harry posed for a picture! Harry was pleased with the cartoon – it made him look very handsome.

Then it was time for a boat ride on the River Seine.

Two boats in two days, thought Harry Stevenson. *I AM a lucky guinea pig.* The Smiths sat at the front and got a good view from the boat's big windows as they ate lunch. Harry perched on Billy's lap and peered ahead, hoping to catch a glimpse of the Eiffel Tower. Billy had shown him a picture of it in Mrs Smith's guidebook. Harry didn't spot the Tower, but as the boat passed under a bridge, the people looking down from it spotted *him.*

'*Oh, regarde, un petit cochon d'Inde!*' they cried, waving and smiling. Harry knew that *cochon d'Inde* was French for guinea pig. He felt like he was famous!

Sightseeing was so much fun that the day

flew past, and soon the Smiths felt hungry again. Mrs Smith got out her guidebook. She was looking for two things – a *crêperie* where the Smiths could eat pancakes, and a food market where they could buy vegetables for Harry. Luckily both were easy to find – just round the corner in a little square. Mr and Mrs Smith weren't very good at speaking French, but they tried their best, and bought a big bunch of carrots, still with their green bushy tops.

Billy held Harry up to the stall-holder, who seemed charmed to see a *cochon d'Inde* and picked out his best spinach leaves to go with the carrots. *Mmmm*, thought

Harry as he wolfed them down. *Mrs Smith was right, French food is excellent.*

Next to the food market was a snug-looking crêperie. It was cosy inside, so the Smiths sank down gratefully into comfy chairs. Harry Stevenson snuggled in Billy's bag and listened as the family decided what to have in their pancakes. His whiskers twitched with excitement when Mr Smith ordered one with spinach. Yum! (Although, it was a bit of a waste to mix spinach with pancakes, he thought.) Harry hoped there might be a few leaves left over for him, but sadly Mr Smith scoffed the lot.

'Right,' said Mrs Smith when everyone

had finished. 'That was delicious. There's just one more thing that will make today perfect – a Christmas market!'

Mr Smith and Billy didn't look too keen, but Mrs Smith had already headed to the door.

'Come on,' she said. 'Let's go!'

CHAPTER 8

A beret,
Harry Stevenson?

The Smiths stepped on to the street, but
stopped in their tracks. Paris looked so
different from earlier in the day. It was late
afternoon now, and the sky was getting
darker. One by one, a million glowing
lights were flickering into life. There were
lights everywhere Harry Stevenson looked:

strings of them draped around the trees, above the streets, up the sides of buildings, and across the bridges over the River Seine. It was like diamonds had been shaken all over the city.

Oohing and *aahing* as they went, the Smiths headed for the Metro, the city's underground railway. Billy used a map in the station to find their route to the Christmas market, following the different coloured Metro lines on the map with his finger. *Am I the first guinea pig down here?* wondered Harry, as he sat next to Billy on a train. It didn't take long to whizz under Paris, and

soon the family were walking up the steps from the Metro. They could hear music, laughter and chatter nearby.

Harry looked around when they reached the top. He saw a village of white tents, with crowds of people milling about.

'The Christmas market!' cried Mrs Smith, marching forward. 'Come on!' she called to Mr Smith and Billy.

Harry sniffed the air. There were fine smells coming from the market. Billy and Mr Smith must have noticed them too, as they hurried after Mrs Smith.

Soon the family was deep in the happy crowd. Harry looked out from Billy's bag as they moved from stall to stall, enjoying everything they saw – and tasted!

It was hard for Harry not to feel hungry as the Smiths tried everything on offer. Even though they'd had lots of pancakes, the market food was too good to miss. There were hot roasted chestnuts, gingerbread Christmas trees, candied fruit, pastries and cookies. Clouds of steam billowed from the stalls as chefs stirred giant cauldrons of onion soup, and dished up big plates of sliced potato, cheese and bacon. Harry wished there was a stall selling food for him too. His stomach growled.

As the Smiths made their way through the market they passed some stalls where traders were shutting up for the day. Harry could see a greengrocer starting to pack vegetables away. He gazed hungrily at the display of carrots, cabbages and sprouts. Harry *did* like sprouts.

'That's just the normal, daytime bit of the market,' said Mrs Smith. 'We can see those things anytime. Look, there are more Christmassy stalls over there.'

Oh, that's a shame, thought Harry Stevenson, disappointed.

The Smiths moved on. There was so much to see! They looked at wooden toys, pottery, woven baskets, jewellery, Christmas decorations and all sorts of clothing. Harry listened as his family discussed what to buy. He tried to be interested but his mind kept wandering back to those sprouts. By the time the Smiths reached a hat stall, he was feeling very hungry indeed.

'Let's all buy a hat!' said Mrs Smith. 'It'll keep us warm AND be a souvenir. I've always fancied wearing a beret.'

Harry watched as his family tried on hats. Then he watched as they tried on some more. There were a *lot* of hats to consider. Mr Smith thought he suited a trilby, although he quite liked a flat cap too. Mrs

Smith looked swish in a furry beret, but she couldn't decide which colour to get – or whether she should buy some furry gloves to match. As for Billy, he'd spotted a large rack of bobble hats in the shape of animals and was trying on every one.

By now Harry was feeling bored as well as hungry. Billy had put his bag down, making it easy for Harry to jump out on to the floor. As usual, Harry's greedy stomach rowed with Harry's sensible brain about whether that would be a good idea or not – and, as ever, Harry's stomach won! *They'll be here for ages yet*, Harry thought. *I'll just nip over to the sprouts, have a quick nibble, and be back in the time it takes Mrs Smith to choose a hat.*

So Harry leaped out of the bag and scuttled under the stalls! He was soon at the vegetable stand. The grocer was dealing with his last few customers, so Harry wasted no time in scoffing as many sprouts and carrots as possible. He crouched down behind a box of sprouts and enjoyed a feast.

Fantastique, thought Harry, his mouth full of sprouts. *Right, I'd better find the Smiths again. They MUST have chosen their hats by now.*

Harry darted back through the market to the hat stand.

But when he got back there, the Smiths had gone.

He looked all around. The Smiths were nowhere to be seen.

Harry Stevenson was lost in Paris!

CHAPTER 9

Oh, no,
Harry Stevenson!

Harry Stevenson raced through the Christmas market, running here and there as he searched for the Smiths. He was careful to stay hidden as he didn't want to get into even *more* trouble.

I must find Billy, thought Harry.

Then – at last! Harry spotted a trio of

people, some way ahead of him. He couldn't see their faces but they were wearing a beret, a trilby and a bobble hat. The Smiths! Harry raced after his family. It seemed to take ages to reach them – he had to keep dodging out of people's way or hiding under market stalls to catch his breath.

The Smiths headed out of the market into some nearby gardens, leaving its hustle and bustle behind. Soon the noise of the market had faded altogether. The gardens were quiet and lit by moonlight. The family stopped for a moment, meaning Harry could finally catch up.

'WHEEK, WHEEK, WHEEK!' called Harry Stevenson to them. **'WHEEK, WHEEK, WHEEK!'**

The family turned – but to Harry's dismay, he saw they weren't the Smiths! He'd been following some strangers! He ducked out of sight into the shadows, not wanting to be seen by anyone but the Smiths. The family looked around, confused. Then they set off again, leaving Harry by himself in the cold.

Harry Stevenson tiptoed out of the shadows and on to some grass. *Where are you, Billy?* He stood on his hind legs and peered across the gardens, but couldn't spot his friend anywhere. Could he smell him, instead? *Sniff, sniff, sniff.* There was no scent of Billy, though – just a cool, fresh kind of smell, which made Harry think of clouds and water.

Something tiny and white drifted on to Harry's nose. It was a snowflake. Harry Stevenson had only seen snowflakes on TV before. Now one was melting on his fur! Soon more flakes fell, quicker and heavier. Harry looked up into the black, inky sky and saw billions of feathery dots tumbling and swirling towards him. On and on they came, falling silently in the dark. Harry gazed in wonder. Another snowflake landed on his furry nose and he licked it off. *This must be what the sky tastes like*, he thought. Harry gave a small popcorn of excitement, thrilled to taste something so strange. He kicked up his paws and danced in the snow.

It didn't take long for the snow to cover the ground. Harry crouched under a bench and shivered. It was getting colder, and water from the melted snowflakes was freezing on his whiskers. Now the snow didn't seem quite so special. *I must find somewhere warm and dry,* thought Harry. *Billy will never find me here.* So off he ran, flitting through the shadows on quick, chilly paws. He hid under bushes, ducked below bins and scuttled behind fences. People passed within a whisker's length, but never looked down to spot the little creature below them – in fact, everyone seemed to be staring up. They were pointing at something far above.

Harry followed their gaze up, up, up . . .

and up some more.

Harry Stevenson stopped in his tracks. He blinked snow from his eyes and stared in amazement. Looming up ahead, like a massive pointy spaceship, was a huge structure, ablaze with lights. It was so big that Harry felt dizzy. He crouched down with fear, his little heart beating fast. *It didn't look that size in the guidebook,* he thought. For there, in front of him, so much bigger in real life, was something he'd been looking for all day – the Eiffel Tower!

CHAPTER 10

Who's that, Harry Stevenson?

This is what an ant must feel like when it first sees a house, thought Harry Stevenson. Harry didn't enjoy feeling ant-like, so he lowered his gaze to the ground. Under the Eiffel Tower's great arches was a vast space, as big as the Sparky FC stadium, and in that space Harry spied a Christmas tree. The tree would have looked giant anywhere else, but here it seemed as small as the one in the Smiths' flat. Next to the tree was some sort of shed, which glowed with a cosy-looking light. Harry Stevenson shivered. *Brrr.* The shed would be the perfect place to shelter until Billy found him, Harry decided.

Harry scampered through the snow to the Tower, trying not to look up. He didn't want to feel dizzy again. Soon he'd reached its base and took a quick look around. When the coast was clear, he darted across to the shed. The front of the shed was just a low fence for some reason, but Harry didn't stop to see why. He just needed to get into the warm! Harry wriggled through a gap in the walls and breathed a sigh of relief. Now he was safe from the cold. Even better, the shed was full of one of his favourite things: hay!

Harry chose a quiet spot and snuggled down gratefully. There was a musky smell in the air, but he felt too cold to worry about it. He nibbled the last bits of snow off his fur, and brushed the melted ice from his whiskers. *Phew, that's better,* he thought, heating up as he munched on a strand of hay. The hay was delicious. Harry could almost feel the warmth of sunny meadows flow into his body. He smacked his lips, just like someone tasting wine. *Mmmmm!* sighed Harry. *I'm getting gold and honey flavours*

. . . a hint of lavender . . . and top notes of clover and daisies.

As Harry chomped on the hay, he became aware that he was eating very noisily. A loud chewing sound filled the shed. *I must be REALLY hungry to make such a racket,* he thought. Harry tried to be quieter, but the sound continued. There was some loud breathing too. *Strange.* Harry stopped eating, and cocked his head to listen. There it was again! *Well, that's very odd,* thought Harry. *If I'M not making the noise – who is?*

Harry took a look around.

Oh.

Harry Stevenson wasn't alone in the shed. Instead, he was sharing it with some large and decidedly musky-smelling shapes. Harry squinted at the shapes. It took a while to work out what they were – and even then, he needed to look again, just to make sure. He blinked a few times, in case there was still snow in his eyes – but, no, he was right. *Well,* thought Harry Stevenson. *I never expected to see THAT in Paris.* He studied the shapes curiously, taking in their shaggy pelts, their grand, branch-like antlers . . . and gentle reindeer faces!

Harry had watched enough nature shows

with Billy to know that reindeer lived in wild, snowy lands far away – so what were they doing in a city like Paris? Did reindeer have city breaks too? Luckily the reindeer didn't seem to mind Harry scoffing their hay, and carried on chewing noisily. But the mystery deepened as Harry realized he too was being watched. Next to the reindeer was a big, carved chair – and in that chair sat a man, looking down at Harry with twinkly eyes. Normally, Harry would have shrunk into the hay with fear, but he didn't feel scared at all. The man had a kind face and seemed strangely familiar. *Hmm*, puzzled Harry. *Have I seen him before in a film?* He looked the man up and down, hunting for

clues. *White beard, red coat, jolly face . . .*
Hang on . . .
Is that . . . FATHER CHRISTMAS?!

CHAPTER 11

Happy Christmas, Harry Stevenson?

Harry Stevenson gazed at Father Christmas, a strand of hay dangling from his mouth. *Getting lost, reindeer, Father Christmas* – it was all too much for a tired little guinea pig. And, as if that wasn't enough, the sound of laughter was now coming from the front of the shed. Harry turned around. There was a group of children leaning over the fence. They were excited about something and were giggling and pointing. With a start, Harry saw they were pointing at HIM!

Harry was causing a bit of a stir. Well, it *is* quite unusual to see a guinea pig in a Christmas display. As more people spotted the excitement, the crowd around Santa's Grotto (for that is what the 'shed' was) grew and grew. Soon people were taking photographs with their phones. Cameras flashed and dazzled Harry's eyes. *Flee*, said Harry's brain – but where to? He was so confused he couldn't think properly. Then – thank goodness! Harry heard a voice he knew and loved.

'HARRY!' called the voice, and Harry looked towards it. There in the crowd was a face he loved: Billy's!

Harry ran towards the fence, but it was too high for him to jump over. Billy wasn't tall enough to reach down to get him, either. As Harry looked up at Billy, he saw his friend's eyes widen with surprise – and felt gentle hands pick him up.

'WHEEEK, WHEEK, WHEEK!' sang Harry Stevenson joyfully. For he knew exactly what was happening. Father Christmas was handing him to Billy!

Back in their hotel room, the Smiths were enjoying mugs of rich, creamy *chocolat chaud*. They were lying on the enormous hotel bed together, with Harry sitting on a pillow.

'Only YOU could get lost in Paris, Harry,' laughed Billy. Harry chirruped in reply. He felt very glad to be back with his family – especially as they'd bought him some sprouts from the Christmas market.

'What shall we do tomorrow, then?' asked Mrs Smith, reaching for her guidebook. 'Another market, maybe?'

'Erm, I've got a suggestion,' said Mr Smith. And he handed Billy an envelope. 'Here's an early Christmas present, Billy. I hope you like it.'

Harry watched as Billy opened the envelope. What could be inside?

'WOW, DAD, THANKS!!' yelled Billy. 'That's amazing!'

He held up three tickets to the Sparky FC versus PSG match! They were really good seats too – in a box, with a meal as well, thrown in by Sparky FC as a thank you for Harry's winning goal and crime-fighting exploits. Harry was invited too, of course.

'You don't mind this instead of a market, Mum?' asked Billy anxiously.

Harry looked towards Mrs Smith. What would she say? But to Harry's surprise, Mrs Smith gave a great big smile.

'Of course not, Billy,' she said. 'And to be honest, I've probably seen enough markets for a while after today's drama.'

'Your mum knew all along,' winked Mr Smith. 'She was just pretending not to, in case we spoiled the surprise.'

Mrs Smith knows EVERYTHING, thought Harry admiringly.

What a trip it had been! And there was even more to look forward to tomorrow. The Smiths lay back and sighed happily.

'Father Christmas reuniting us was the best Christmas present ever,' smiled Billy, as he stroked Harry's nose.

Harry Stevenson had to agree.

Although . . . the sprouts *definitely* came a close second.

Happy Christmas, Harry Stevenson!

THE END

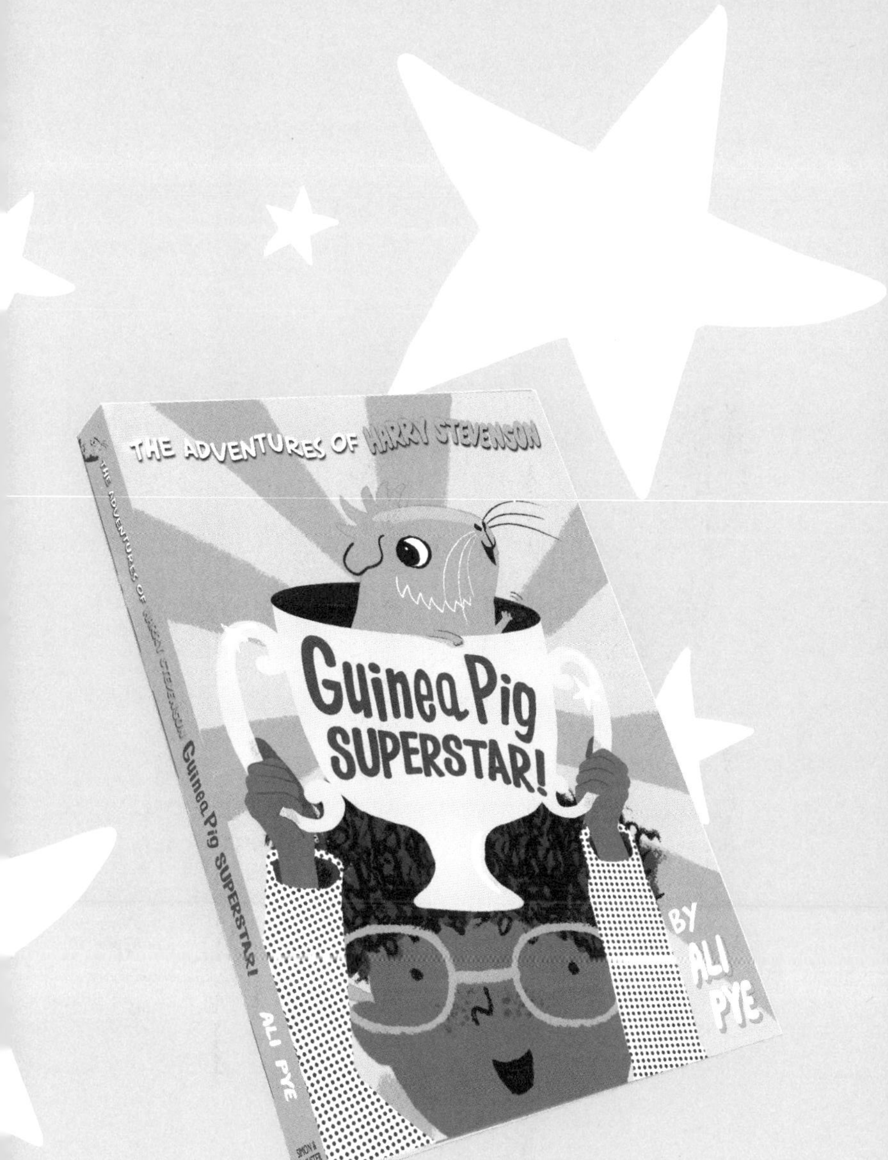

Ali Pye is the author and illustrator of
The Adventures of Harry Stevenson.
These books were inspired by a real-life
guinea pig (who turned out to be a girl
and was re-named Harriet Stevenson).
She lives in Twickenham with her husband,
children, two guinea pigs: Beryl and
Badger, and Saffy the dog.